00-1 |01-1 02 | 04-1 05-1 1 1

ORANGE CITY PUBLIC LIBRARY
Orange City, IA

1. Items are returnable on the date printed on the due date slip in this pocket. Items may be renewed once except books on reserve.

2. Magazines may be kept one week and may be renewed once for the same period.

3. A fine of five cents a day will be charged on each item which is not returned on its due date.

4. All injuries to any library materials beyond reasonable wear, and all losses shall be made good to the satisfaction of the Librarian

DEMCO

KIDS CAN'T STOP READING THE CHOOSE YOUR OWN ADVENTURE® STORIES!

"Choose Your Own Adventure is the best thing that has come along since books themselves."

—Alysha Beyer, age 11

"I didn't read much before, but now I read my Choose Your Own Adventure books almost every night."

—Chris Brogan, age 13

"I love the control I have over what happens next."

—Kosta Efstathiou, age 17

"Choose Your Own Adventure books are so much fun to read and collect—I want them all!"

—Brendan Davin, age 11

And teachers like this series, too:

"We have read and reread, worn thin, loved, loaned, bought for others, and donated to school libraries our Choose Your Own Adventure books."

CHOOSE YOUR OWN ADVENTURE®— AND MAKE READING MORE FUN!

CHOOSE YOUR OWN ADVENTURE®
titles in Large-Print Editions:

#66 SECRET OF THE NINJA
#88 MASTER OF KUNG FU
#92 RETURN OF THE NINJA
#97 THROUGH THE BLACK HOLE
#98 YOU ARE A MILLIONAIRE
#100 THE WORST DAY OF YOUR LIFE
#101 ALIEN, GO HOME!
#102 MASTER OF TAE KWAN DO
#106 HIJACKED!
#108 MASTER OF KARATE
#110 INVADERS FROM WITHIN
#112 SKATEBOARD CHAMPION
#114 DAREDEVIL PARK
#117 THE SEARCH FOR ALADDIN'S LAMP
#118 VAMPIRE INVADERS
#120 GHOST TRAIN
#121 BEHIND THE WHEEL
#122 MAGIC MASTER
#124 SUPERBIKE
#138 DINOSAUR ISLAND

All-Time Best-Sellers!

CHOOSE YOUR OWN ADVENTURE® • 124

SUPERBIKE

BY EDWARD PACKARD

ILLUSTRATED BY JUDITH MITCHELL

Orange City Public Library
112 Albany Ave. S.E.
Orange City, IA 51041-0346

Gareth Stevens Publishing
MILWAUKEE

For a free color catalog describing Gareth Stevens' list of high-quality books, call 1-800-542-2595 (USA) or 1-800-461-9120 (Canada). Gareth Stevens' Fax: (414) 225-0377.

Library of Congress Cataloging-in-Publication Data

Packard, Edward.
Superbike/by Edward Packard; illustrated by
Judith Mitchell.
p. cm. — (Choose your own adventure; 124)
Summary: The reader's decisions control the course of an adventure
in which a specially designed Superbike, capable of incredible speed,
may fall into the wrong hands.
ISBN 0-8368-1407-X
1. Plot-your-own stories. [1. Bicycles and bicycling—Fiction.
2. Adventure and adventurers—Fiction. 3. Plot-your-own stories.]
I. Mitchell, Judith, 1951- ill. II. Title. III. Series.
PZ7.P1245Sw 1995
[Fic]—dc20 95-21668

This edition first published in 1995 by
Gareth Stevens Publishing
1555 North RiverCenter Drive, Suite 201
Milwaukee, Wisconsin 53212 USA

CHOOSE YOUR OWN ADVENTURE® is a trademark of Bantam Doubleday Dell Books for Young Readers, a division of Bantam Doubleday Dell Publishing Group, Inc.

Original conception of Edward Packard.
Interior illustrations by Judith Mitchell. Cover art by Catherine Huerta.

© 1992 by Edward Packard. Cover art and interior illustrations © 1992 by Bantam Books. Published by arrangement with Bantam Doubleday Dell Books for Young Readers, a division of Bantam Doubleday Dell Publishing Group, Inc.

All rights to this edition reserved to Gareth Stevens, Inc. No part of this book may be reproduced, stored in a retrieval system, or transmitted in any form or by any means, electronic, mechanical, photocopying, recording, or otherwise without the prior written permission of the publisher except for the inclusion of brief quotations in an acknowledged review.

Printed in the United States of America

1 2 3 4 5 6 7 8 9 99 98 97 96 95

SUPERBIKE

TOUR OF AMERICA
WINNER
$20,000
$20,000

WARNING!!!

Do not read this book straight through from beginning to end. These pages contain many different adventures that you may have when a scientific genius lets you test his latest invention, the Superbike.

From time to time as you read along, you'll have a chance to make a choice. After you make your decision, follow the instructions to find out what happens to you next.

On the Superbike, you may have a chance to win a cross-country bike race and become rich and famous. But be careful. There are people out there who would like to get their hands on the Superbike—any way they can.

Good luck!

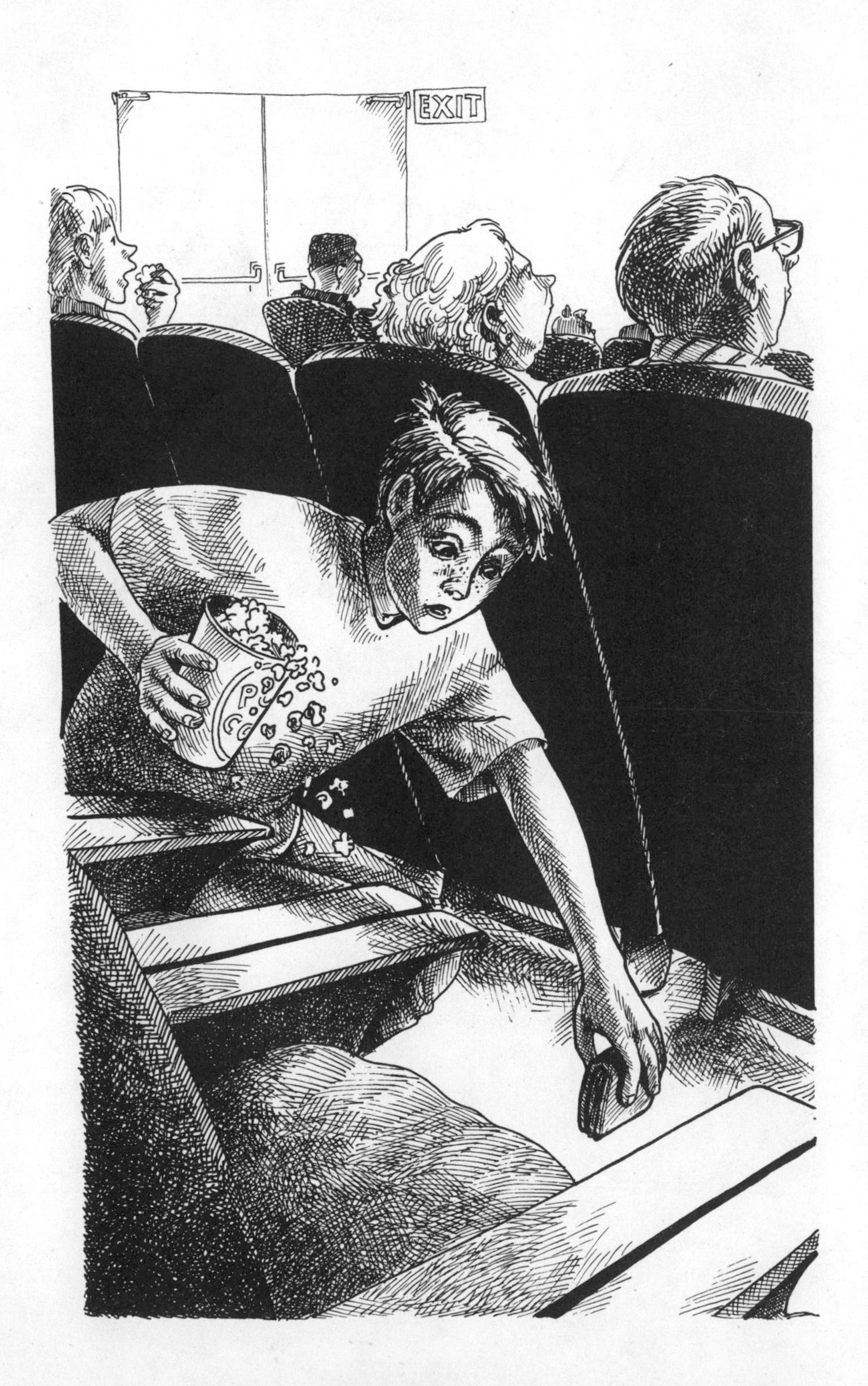
EXIT

You've just settled down in your seat at the movie theater. The house lights have darkened, and the show is about to begin. As you reach into your popcorn bucket, you move your foot a little and kick something. You reach down. It's a wallet. There's no one in any of the nearby seats—it must have fallen out of someone's pocket at an earlier show.

When the lights come on after the movie, you look inside the wallet. It contains over three hundred dollars in cash along with some credit cards, a driver's license, and a scrap of paper with what look like mathematical formulas written on it. The driver's license belongs to Dr. Aaron Kepler, of 330 Wildwood Road.

For an instant you think about how nice it would be to have three hundred dollars, but you put that thought out of your mind quickly. When you get home, you call information to get Dr. Kepler's number. You dial it and after several rings, a voice answers.

"Dr. Kepler?" you say.

"Yes?"

"I think I found your wallet—it was under my seat at the movies."

"Oh, thank you, thank you," he says, almost shouting. "You can't imagine how important that wallet is to me."

"Sure I can," you say. "Three hundred dollars is a lot of money."

"It's not that—not that at all," he says. "Where are you?"

Turn to page 2.

2

You give Dr. Kepler your address. He says he'll be over right away. His house is only a couple of miles from yours. As you wait for him to arrive, you wonder whether he will give you a reward. From the way he sounded, the money wasn't the most important thing in his wallet.

As you are thinking about how you would spend the reward money, the doorbell rings. You open it, and the man standing on the front steps introduces himself as Dr. Kepler. He's a small, spindly man with frizzy brown hair. One of his legs is shorter than the other, and he walks with the aid of a cane. "Thank you," he says, practically ripping the wallet out of your hand. He opens it and pulls out the scrap of paper with the mathematical formulas on it and lets the wallet drop to the floor. "Still here!" he says. "How could I have been so stupid as to let it out of my hand!"

You pick up the wallet and hold it out. Dr. Kepler takes it. "Yes, I'll need these other things," he says. For the first time he looks at you. He smiles and holds out his hand. "Thank you so much," he says.

"You're welcome." You're thinking that if he's going to offer you a reward, now would be the time to do it.

"I'm a lucky man," he says. "Not just because I got my wallet back, but also because I found a person I know I can trust." He looks at the formulas again and then folds the paper carefully and puts it in his jacket pocket. "You see, I need an honest person to try out my latest invention."

Go on to the next page.

"What kind of invention?" you ask Dr. Kepler.

"You can see for yourself. Can you come to my laboratory Saturday morning at ten o'clock? It's only a couple of miles from here."

"Sure. I'll come over on my bike."

Dr. Kepler strokes his chin for a moment, looking thoughtful. Then he says, "Walk, even though it takes longer. I'm going to give you a bike to ride home—a bike you'll like a lot better than the one you have."

"Great," you say. "I'll be there."

"Good. See you Saturday. My address is 330 Wildwood Road. I'll be in my laboratory. It's the building just behind my house." Dr. Kepler turns and starts for the door without another word. You watch him patting his jacket pocket as he walks to his car.

You're pleased, of course, but rather puzzled. Is Dr. Kepler really going to give you a new bike as a reward? And what could his invention be?

That Saturday you walk to Dr. Kepler's laboratory, which is located in a converted barn behind his house. As soon as Dr. Kepler opens the door, you see a shiny new bike standing in the middle of the floor. It's a beauty—low and streamlined, with just three flat spokes on each wheel. It's painted blue. Not an ordinary blue, but a shining, glimmering greenish blue.

Turn to page 24.

You don't look back. Still, his comment worries you. You hope that he gets interested in something else besides you and your bike, and soon.

For a while it seems that your wish has come true. You don't even see Fred or his friend Mack for a couple of weeks. Then one day as you're biking home, you stop to wait for a light to change. Suddenly Fred and Mack jump out from behind a parked car. Each of them is carrying a long stick. Fred shoves his stick between the spokes of your front wheel.

If you push off fast, you might succeed in flipping the stick out of his hand and getting away. On the other hand, he might succeed in tripping you up and spilling your bike!

If you try to get away, turn to page 50.

If you decide to talk to them, turn to page 34.

Just then a call comes in. "All points—this is Officer Riddley on foot patrol on Young's Hill Road. Just saw a bike going up the hill that fits the description."

"We're on our way," Soria says. He flips on his siren and flashing light and performs a neat U-turn. In a minute you're racing toward Young's Hill Road.

"You'll really have to step on it," you say. "That bike will do fifty miles an hour."

"It won't do fifty going up Young's Hill," Soria says. "We'll get him."

The police car screams across Main Street and onto Young's Hill Road. Soria presses the gas pedal to the floor as he races up the steep slope.

"There he is," you say. "Near the top. We'll catch him before he starts down!"

The thief sees the car coming. He steers the bike over to the edge of the road. There's nothing but a cliff there, with a hundred-foot drop onto the rocks below.

"He's trapped now," you say. "We've got him."

Soria pulls the police car to a stop a few yards away from the thief, who's standing near the edge of the cliff. The Superbike is next to him.

"Keep low, kid," the officer orders. "This could get rough."

Turn to page 29.

"That's a danger," he says. "But if this bike is ever taken from you, I'll know it wasn't your fault, because you've already proven to me that you're honest."

"Okay, I'll try it," you say. "And thanks for choosing me. But first tell me—what does the air magnet do?"

Dr. Kepler nods. "Do you know what keeps a bike from going faster than it does?" he asks.

"You can only pedal so fast," you say.

"That's one reason," he says. "There are three others. One is the friction of the moving parts, and another is the friction of the tires against the road. A high-tech racing bike reduces these to almost nothing. The third and most important factor is air resistance. The faster you go, the faster the wind blows against you."

"Does the air magnet change that?"

"Exactly. The air magnet sends out a stream of charges that repulse air molecules. The air coming at the bike is diverted to the sides. Riding the Superbike is like riding with the wind always at your back, blowing at the same speed that you're moving."

"I can't wait to try it," you say.

Turn to page 30.

You hold up a hand to show you've heard him. Then you wheel around the corner, pedaling lazily while the bike accelerates to twenty miles per hour. You pedal faster, gaining on a car ahead of you. You pass it at thirty-five miles per hour, then glance back to see the look of astonishment on the driver's face.

You keep pedaling, easily maintaining thirty miles per hour. The strange thing is that there's no

wind in your face. You're sure that you could go quite a bit faster, but there's a stop sign about a quarter of a mile ahead. You decide that you'd better try the brakes before you do anything else.

Go on to the next page.

10

First you try the regular brakes, just to make sure they work. Then you twist the knob on the air magnet. Suddenly you feel the wind in your face. The air magnet is attracting instead of repulsing the air. The Superbike quickly and smoothly slows down.

You coast to the side of the road and hop off. The car you passed earlier goes by. The driver practically drives off the road—he can't keep his eyes off your bike.

Turn to page 110.

A week has passed. Fred and Mack are on probation at school. They've both been warned that the next time they won't get off so easily. You've got your air magnet back, but you can't figure out how to rehook it to your bike.

You call Dr. Kepler to tell him what happened. A woman's voice answers the phone.

"Is Dr. Kepler in?" you ask.

"I'm afraid not," the woman says in a low tone. "I'm Dr. Kepler's sister. Dr. Kepler had a heart attack three days ago and he's in the hospital. He probably won't be home for a long time."

"I'm really sorry to hear that," you say. "I'll talk to him when he's feeling better." You hang up the phone. Then you go out to the garage and stand looking at your bike. It's the best bike in town, but you sure wish it were still a Superbike.

The End

You decide that you can trust your friends to keep quiet about the Superbike. The next Monday you ride the Superbike to school. As you pedal up to the school yard, you adjust the airflow so that it's the same as it would be with a normal bike. When school lets out, you show your new bike to your friends. They are all impressed by it, even without knowing about the air magnet. Your friend Tim Martin, who just got a racing bike for his birthday, asks if you want to race.

You say, "Well, I don't know. You've been training a lot, Tim."

"Ah, come on," he says. "I'll race you to the pizza parlor. It's about two miles with a steep hill on the way. Perfect course to test out your new bike." Tim has one foot over his bike, ready to push off.

"Well, okay," you say.

Turn to page 22.

One day you're traveling along, doing about forty-five, when a car passes you. The person in the passenger seat waves at you. It's Ronnie Drayton, a kid in your class. You slow down, and the car is soon out of sight. But the next day when you get to school you discover that Ronnie has told everyone that he and his mother clocked you going forty-five miles per hour. When school lets out, everyone in your class crowds around you as you unlock your bike. Some older kids are there, too, including a couple of big guys named Fred Lester and Mack Krieg who are known for pushing people around.

Naturally, everyone wants to know how your bike can go so fast. You just keep saying, "It's a real good bike."

No one is satisfied with that answer, and you can't blame them. Still, you're determined not to give away the secret.

You get on the bike and head out. As you're pulling out of the school grounds, Fred Lester yells after you, "We'll find out one way or another!"

Turn to page 4.

The race will be covered on national TV. Several large companies are sponsoring the event, and the grand prize is one hundred thousand dollars. The more you think about the Tour of America, the more determined you are to enter it and win.

You start reading up on biking and training. On weekends you take your bike out on longer and longer runs. Your goal is not to see how fast you can go but to build up your endurance and learn to shift smoothly every time.

One day you realize that you had better check to make sure that using the air magnet is legal in competition. You send away for a copy of the rules used in the big bike tours. Rule number 7 states that no bike will be allowed to use a motor or engine of any kind. You don't know exactly how the air magnet works, but it's certainly not a motor or an engine since it doesn't use fuel or have any moving parts. Therefore your Superbike is perfectly legal, and that means you could be in for some really big prize money!

Turn to page 36.

Fear grips you. In the same instant some instinct tells you to turn the knob on the air magnet all the way to the left. Now, instead of no wind blowing in your face, you're attracting air—a gale blowing against you and the bike, breaking your fall. A second later you land softly in the ravine.

You pick up your bike and start climbing back up to the road. Tim has stopped at the edge of the embankment and is looking down at you.

"Wow," he says. "I can't believe you can still walk after that spill."

"No problem," you say, leaping back onto the shoulder of the road.

Tim looks at your bike. "It's not even scratched."

"Yeah, it's really something," you say, and a split second later you're on it again, speeding toward the pizza parlor. Tim races to catch up, but you beat him easily.

"Well, you won after all," he says as he pulls up beside you.

You shake your head. "You would have won if you hadn't stopped to see how I was, so I'll buy you a soda." The two of you sit down in a booth and order sodas. While you're waiting for them to arrive, you and Tim talk about the race.

Go on to the next page.

"Hey, how about letting me try your bike?" Tim says. "I'd be real careful with it."

You're not surprised that Tim wants to borrow the Superbike. He's a good friend, and you'd like to let him try it, but you don't know if it's a good idea. After all, it's the only bike of its kind in the world. You're not sure you want to let it out of your hands, even for a few minutes.

If you let Tim ride the Superbike,
turn to page 32.

If you decide not to let him ride it,
turn to page 27.

COUCH POTATO VIDEO
433

At five after twelve, Tim nudges you and points toward the video rental place. "That's him, leaning that bike up against the outside of the building. I'll go phone the police." He hurries toward the pay phone in the back of the store.

You step outside and stare at the bike the thief left. It's been painted recently, but you see a cone-shaped object in the middle of the handlebars. It's the Superbike, all right.

You know the thief will probably be in the video store only long enough to drop off the tape. Tim's still on the phone—you can't wait for him. This could be your only chance to get your bike back. You've got to do something.

Maybe you could get to the bike before the thief does and ride off. But you hate to think what he might do if he catches you. Maybe you should just try to take his picture and get the videotape he returned so the police can fingerprint it.

If you try to escape on the Superbike,
turn to page 43.

If you try to take the thief's picture and get his fingerprints, turn to page 26.

Tim looks as if he's trying not to cry. "A guy took it. I was coming down Auburn Road on the way here. The bike was really traveling. I passed this pickup truck going about forty miles an hour. Then I stopped for a red light. The driver screeched up beside me and jumped out. Before I knew what was happening he grabbed the bike and knocked me down. He said, 'You're not going to pass me on that again.' Then he threw the bike in the back of his truck and drove off."

You feel like yelling, but you say, "Tim, did you get his license number?"

"Yeah, it's JS 2253." Tim then describes the thief as an average-sized man about twenty years old with curly brown hair and a mole on his right cheek.

"Come with me while I call the police," you say.

The police officer you talk to promises to track down the thief. Later he calls and tells you that the pickup truck with the license plate Tim memorized was recently stolen, and that another officer just found it in an empty lot.

"Please put out an alarm for the bike," you say. "The thief must have used it to get away with."

"We'll keep an eye out," the officer says, "but most likely he'll keep it out of sight. Thieves don't ride very far with stolen bikes."

"He might have ridden far on this one," you say. "It's a Superbike."

Turn to page 42.

Bike camp begins on June 2 and lasts a month. The moment you arrive you feel you've made a good choice. Squaw Valley, nestled in the Sierra Nevada mountains, is a beautiful area. You and about fifty other young bikers will be housed in a ski lodge that's empty now in the off-season. The coaching staff is made up of former world-class racers, including the Austrian biker Werner Haupt, who won the Tour de France two years in a row.

You soon make friends with several of the other bikers, even though you're the youngest one in the camp. Some of the more experienced racers are skeptical that you could even finish, much less win, the Tour of America.

At breakfast the first morning, a biker at your table named Thad Williams tells you that this is his second year at the camp. He warns that the first day of practice will include a twenty-mile stretch with several long, steep slopes. "Anyone who doesn't finish in two hours may be sent home," he says.

You chuckle. You're not worried about making the time.

"Don't laugh," Thad says. "Some of those hills are wicked. And another problem is navigation. You have to follow a map, and if you make a wrong turn, you're almost certain to miss the deadline."

"Maybe we could ride along together," you say.

This time it's Thad who chuckles. "Sure, if you can keep up with me," he says.

Turn to page 41.

The moment the words are out of your mouth, Tim is off—racing along the level stretch of road between the school and the first hill. You push off after him, and the Superbike glides forward, gradually picking up speed.

Tim has shifted into high gear—he's hit thirty miles per hour by now. Thanks to his head start and hard pedaling, he's opened up a hundred-yard lead.

You pedal hard, upshifting several times. At twenty miles per hour you activate the air magnet. The wind blowing in your face seems to die, as if you were suddenly in front of a strong tail wind. The Superbike accelerates with ease. You reach twenty-five miles per hour, then thirty, then thirty-five. You're gaining rapidly on Tim as he reaches the bottom of the steep hill.

Turn to page 38.

Instead of answering, you pedal harder.

Thad is showing his stuff, too, riding through the pack as if it were standing still. By the top of the long upgrade, he's in the lead. He doesn't look around until he reaches the peak of the slope. Then he glances back and sees that you're right behind him.

You can see the shocked look on his face. You know that he probably thought you'd still be in the back of the pack.

"Good biking, kid," he calls over his shoulder. "But you'd better pace yourself. That hill we just climbed is flat compared to what's ahead."

On the next stretch you take it easy. You know you're not as strong or in as good condition as most of the other bikers, and you want to save your energy for the steep climb that lies ahead. Thad Williams is still the only biker ahead of you as you start creeping up a very steep stretch of road.

Your air magnet isn't much use going up steep hills, because gravity is the big problem, rather than air resistance. By the time you reach the top, two other bikers have passed you. Thad, now on the downside of the hill, has opened up his lead even more.

"Okay, Superbike," you say, shifting and adjusting the air magnet. "Let's go."

Turn to page 44.

You gaze admiringly at the bike.

"Notice anything unusual about it?" Dr. Kepler asks.

"It sure looks fast," you say.

"It is, but that's not what I meant. Pick it up."

You walk over, grab hold of the frame, and lift the bike right over your head. "Wow—it's so light!"

You stand back to admire the bike from a distance. "This is no ordinary bike," you say.

"No indeed," says Dr. Kepler. "And I'm about to make it even less ordinary. I'm about to make it a Superbike."

He takes a small, silver, cone-shaped object out of his pocket and screws it onto the middle of the handlebars. "This is my invention," he says. "I call it the air magnet. It's based on a formula that was in my wallet. It's a formula I don't want to reveal to anyone, because the same principles could be used to make weapons."

"What does the air magnet do?"

Kepler smiles. "That's what you're going to find out for me," he says. "You see, because of my disability I'm not able to ride a bike. I need someone else to test it. It has to be someone I can trust. You are that person."

"Well, I'd love to try it," you say. "But if it's so valuable, I'm not sure I want to be responsible for it. What if it were stolen from me?"

Turn to page 7.

A moment later the thief walks out of the video store. You snap his picture. He sees you. He grabs the bike, hops on, and accelerates toward you. You leap up onto the trunk of a car and snap another picture as he goes by. Then you jump down and race into the video rental place. "What was that tape that just came in?" you ask the clerk. "I've got to have it."

The clerk reaches for the tape, still on the counter.

"Don't touch it!" you say. "It's got fingerprints."

The clerk puts his hand inside a little plastic bag and uses it to pick up the tape. "What's this all about, anyway?" he demands.

"Hold it for me, will you? I'll be right back. And don't touch it—it's got police evidence."

You race out of the store. Two police cars are now in the parking lot, including the unmarked one that had left earlier. Tim is standing next to it, talking to the driver.

You hop in one car as Tim gets into the other. The cops put out an all-points alarm and then cruise around the neighborhood. There's no sign of the thief or your bike. You're not surprised. Considering how fast the Superbike is, you know the thief could be miles away by now.

"Don't worry," Officer Soria tells you as he drives. "With those pictures you took, plus the fingerprints on the tape, we should have no trouble tracking this guy down."

Turn to page 6.

"I'm sorry, Tim," you say, "but I think I'd better not lend this bike out. I promised the man who gave it to me that I'd be extra careful with it."

"Yeah, well, thanks anyway," Tim says. He gets up from the table. "I've got to get going."

You can tell that he's upset. "I'm really sorry," you say again.

"That's okay," he says. "Enjoy the sodas. And have fun with your new bike." He heads for the door.

When your soda comes, you sip it slowly, deep in thought. Owning a Superbike is great, but you can see that it may lead to problems.

After your race with Tim you continue to ride the Superbike to school, but you're careful not to use the air magnet except when you're alone. Still, all the kids can tell that the bike is something special. You're sure that Tim has told people about it. Everyone wants to try it out, but you stick to your rule about not lending it to anyone, even for a few minutes.

You're still eager to see what the Superbike can do, and sometimes after school you ride it out onto the deserted country roads outside of town, where you can really work up some speed. Your strength and endurance improve steadily, and you learn to handle the controls with absolute precision. Almost every time out you set a new speed record, until finally you hit a top speed of forty-eight miles per hour!

Turn to page 14.

You try to keep low, but your curiosity gets the better of you, and you poke your nose over the dashboard. Soria has gotten out of the car, his gun drawn. Police sirens sound behind you. Reinforcements are on the way.

"Hands up," Soria orders the thief.

The man looks at him coldly for a moment. Then he says, "Okay, but if I can't have this bike, then nobody's going to have it." He raises his hands, but with a sudden motion he kicks the bike, sending it spinning into space.

Soria advances on the thief, keeping him covered. "You'll pay all the more dearly for that," he says.

You leap out of the car, run over to the edge of the cliff, and peer down at the crumpled heap of metal and rubber on the rocks below.

The thief will be put away—no doubt about that—but your days with the Superbike are over.

The End

"You can do more than try it," Dr. Kepler says. "The Superbike is yours to keep. It's your reward for your honesty. All I ask is that you call me after you've used it for a while and let me know how it works."

Dr. Kepler throws open the double doors to the laboratory. He hands you a wire bike lock. "That wire is made from a special alloy I developed in my laboratory," he says. "It can't be cut by any shears, or even by a blowtorch." He hands you a tiny slip of paper. "This is the combination to the lock. Memorize it when you get home. Then hide this piece of paper where no one will ever find it." He gestures toward the bike. "To work the air magnet, twist the knob to the right to deflect the air ahead of the bike. By the way, the magnet is coded so it can't be used on any other bike."

You eagerly grab the handlebars and swing one foot over the frame. You twist the knob to the right. You can't wait to see what the Superbike can do!

"The bike has regular brakes," Dr. Kepler continues. "But you can brake even faster by using the air magnet instead. Just twist the knob to the left. That will reverse the airflow."

You hop on the bike and kick off. Even before you've pedaled, the bike has rolled halfway along the driveway. As you start pedaling, it picks up speed quickly.

"Good luck!" Dr. Kepler calls after you.

Turn to page 8.

"Dr. Kepler," you say, "I was as careful as I could be with the bike. I always kept it locked up, and I never let anyone else ride it. Is there any chance you could put another air magnet on it?"

The scientist shakes his head. "I'm not surprised the air magnet was stolen," he says. "You say there were fifty people at the camp. If you have a barrel with fifty apples in it, one of them is bound to be rotten, right?" He gestures with his pipe, his eyes twinkling, and you can't help but smile. "Tell me how the bike did, before this happened," he says.

You describe how you practiced and built up your skills and endurance. Then you tell him that you won a race your first day at bike camp, even though you were the youngest and most inexperienced biker there. You also mention that you reached a top speed of fifty-three miles per hour.

Kepler grins. "So the bike was quite a success?"

"It sure was," you say. "It really was a Superbike."

"Very good," says Kepler. "Then I'm satisfied, and I'll now tell you that I've changed my mind about not licensing my formula for the air magnet. Since I last saw you I had a heart attack. While I was in the hospital, I spent a lot of time thinking. As you know, I was afraid that the principles used in the air magnet might be used to make weapons, and that's something I'm opposed to. But there is another consideration."

Turn to page 51.

"Okay, you can try it," you say. You show him how to work the controls for the air magnet. He watches, wide-eyed. "I'd never believe this unless I'd seen how fast you caught up with me," he says.

Then you let go of the bike, and for the first time Tim notices that it stands by itself, without any support. "Wow, I'd give anything for this bike," he says.

"It's not for sale," you say.

Tim glances at you. "If it were mine, I wouldn't sell it either," he says. "Look, I'll ride it over to your house. You take my bike and we'll meet there."

"Okay," you say. But Tim has already shoved off and is accelerating down the road.

You hop on Tim's bike and follow him. It's a top-notch racing bike, but it's no Superbike. Tim quickly races out of sight, and there's no hope of catching him.

About ten minutes later you reach home. Tim is waiting for you. He's out of breath, as if he'd been running, and there's a horrible look on his face. Your bike is nowhere to be seen.

"Tim, what happened? Where's my bike?"

Turn to page 20.

FAMOUS
PEPPERONI
MUSHROOM
SAUSAGE
PIZZA

You stand over your bike and glare at Mack. "Please take your stick out of my spokes," you say.

"First we want to talk," he says. "What makes this bike go so fast?"

"And don't just say it's a really good bike," Fred says.

"It's specially engineered," you say. "I don't know the technical part—"

"What's this cone-shaped thing?" Fred has his hand on the air magnet. "It has something to do with it, doesn't it?"

"Maybe. I don't really understand how it works."

"Well," says Mack, "we'll find out for you." He reaches into a cloth bag he's carrying and pulls out a pair of heavy-duty wire cutters. While Fred blocks your path, Mack deftly cuts through the mounting of the air magnet. He pockets the device and is about to say something when Fred nudges him. Suddenly they both turn and run. In a moment you see why—a police car has pulled up.

"Officer!"

"I saw it happen," the cop calls to you. He wheels around the corner after Fred and Mack.

Turn to page 11.

You decide to ride your old bike to school and around the neighborhood. If you bring your Superbike to school, everyone will keep pestering you, wanting to ride it. But after school and on weekends you take the Superbike out on the back roads and rev it up to high speeds. Thirty miles per hour is practically coasting for this bike. With a little effort you can get it up to forty, then forty-five, then fifty miles per hour. For a few seconds you hit a new record—fifty-three miles per hour! When cars pass you, the people in them always have the same astonished look on their faces. They can't believe a bike could be going that fast. You know they must be wondering where the motor is.

It's not long before you begin to think about entering some big races and tours. The most important one, coming up the following summer, is the Tour of America. It's destined to be the greatest bike race of all time. It starts on July 1 at noon with an opening lap around Central Park in New York City, then goes across the George Washington Bridge into New Jersey and through a whole string of states to the finish line in Aspen, Colorado.

The race is estimated to take two weeks or more for the leading bikers. Hostels have been set up along the way where the bikers can sleep overnight or rest during the hottest parts of the day. Helicopters over the course will check to make sure none of the bikers are hitching a ride. Millions of people will crowd along the route to watch the bikers race by.

Turn to page 15.

Spring arrives. You're excited about your chances of winning the Tour of America, though you know it's not going to be a piece of cake. After all, your competition will be world-class professional racers, including Pierre Le Beau, the top biker in the world. You'll be riding over all kinds of terrain, in all kinds of weather, day after day. Even with a Superbike you can't expect to win unless you've honed your skills to the utmost.

One day you read in a cycling magazine about a bike-racing training camp in Squaw Valley, California. It might be a good idea to spend a couple of weeks there and get some professional coaching. On the other hand, if you go to bike camp, you'll have to pass up the Tour New England, an important warm-up race for the Tour of America. Getting some practice riding under actual racing conditions might be more valuable than anything a coach could teach you.

If you decide to go to bike camp,
turn to page 21.

If you enter the Tour New England,
turn to page 56.

SQUAW VALLEY CAMP
ALL SEASONS
EARN WITH THE PROS
RACING
GEAR UP
THE ANAEROBIC APPROACH
Q and A:

Tim downshifts gracefully—he's making good speed up the hill—but you've closed the gap to less than five yards.

Soon you draw alongside him, but then he pulls ahead again. You feel yourself getting short of wind as you try to keep up.

Superbike, why aren't we passing him? you think. Then you realize that though you may be riding a Superbike, Tim has been training for bike racing for months, and he's in much better shape than you are. What's more, when you're going uphill like this, wind resistance is not a big factor, so your air magnet isn't much use. You'll have to make up ground on the downhill and flat sections of the course in order to win.

Tim reaches the top of the hill and starts flying down it. By the time you reach the top, he's opened up a two-hundred-yard lead.

The road is a bit rough and gravelly. Your bike would go much faster, but you don't dare. Tim holds his lead all the way down the hill. Only when he reaches the bottom do you start to gain on him. Now you're going to have to fly. It's only a half mile more to the pizza parlor.

Go on to the next page.

You shift smoothly as you pick up speed. Tim's bike is really traveling, but you're gaining ground every second. The Superbike is showing its stuff: thirty-five, forty, then an incredible forty-five miles per hour!

You breeze by Tim. You only have a hundred yards to go, but there's a sharp curve ahead and then an intersection. You've got the right-of-way, but suddenly a car swerves around the corner into your path. You have to swerve too. The Superbike leaves the ground at the curve and flies over an embankment toward the bottom of a ravine.

Turn to page 16.

Later someone tells you that Thad is one of the top bikers in the camp. It's believed that he has a shot at finishing among the leaders in the Tour of America.

At 9:00 A.M. all fifty campers take off down the long access road to the Squaw Valley Ski Area. The weather is perfect, and the bikers are eager to prove themselves. The pace is fast from the beginning, taking advantage of the downhill slope that begins the course. The pack stays grouped pretty closely together for the first couple of miles, until the slope begins to level out.

Thad Williams has been hanging back near the rear of the pack. You've been trailing a few yards behind him, since you agreed to ride together. However, the two of you are so far back that you're beginning to wonder whether he's as much of a hotshot as you've heard.

According to your map, the next five miles will consist of a long, gentle upgrade. Just as the trail begins to curve up, Thad glances over his shoulder at you.

"It's been nice riding with you," he calls out. "But I've got to pick up a little ground now."

He shifts gears and accelerates. In a moment he's passing other bikers right and left. With a grin you activate the air magnet and start pedaling harder. You pick up speed rapidly, shifting down and then up several times. Other bikers give you surprised glances as you go by.

"You'll fade in a hurry at that rate, kid," one of them yells.

Turn to page 23.

Days pass without any word from the police. You feel terrible. It seems as if you've really lost the Superbike. Finally you decide you'd better tell Dr. Kepler what happened. You work up your courage to call him. You're about to pick up the phone when it rings. It's Tim, sounding very excited.

"I saw the bike thief. He was coming out of the video rental place. I was on the school bus when I saw him, so there was no way I could get off and follow him."

"Did he have my bike?"

"No, he was walking. He was carrying a little plastic bag."

"Tim, there was probably a videotape in that bag. He'll have to return it tomorrow—Saturday. We could set up a watch for him."

"We'd better get the cops in on this, too," Tim says.

Turn to page 54.

You race toward the bike. You're just a few feet away from it when the thief walks out of the store. You reach the bike, but it's facing the thief, who is now running toward you. By the time you turn the bike and get going, he'll be close enough to grab you.

Instead of trying to turn the bike, you activate the air magnet to full force. The magnet diverts air in front of the bike, blowing it directly toward the thief. It's not strong enough to stop him, but it startles him for a second, giving you time to mount the bike and ride off. He lunges at you, but it's too late. You speed out of the parking lot.

A police car is coming right at you. You brake hard and swerve. The car screeches to a halt. You whirl and see that the thief has been chasing you, but he's seen the police car and is now running in the other direction.

"That's him!" you yell to the officer.

The officer pulls ahead, trying to close in on the thief.

At that moment the unmarked police car returns, blocking the exit to the lot.

A few minutes later the police have the thief safely handcuffed in the back of a squad car. You've got your Superbike back, and it's as good as new except for a sloppy paint job.

In the weeks ahead you'll have more fun than ever with your Superbike, but you'll be a lot more careful with it, too.

The End

The Superbike flies downhill. Quickly you pass everyone who overtook you on the way up. With about five miles to go, you breeze by Thad, who's beginning to tire from the blistering pace he's set.

You wave as you go by, but he keeps his head down, pedaling hard. By the time he finishes the race, you're settled at a redwood picnic table with your feet up, sipping orange juice and admiring the view of the snowfields near the top of Squaw Mountain.

The other bikers come straggling in. Those who aren't too tired crowd around you.

Mike Tetkoski, the head coach, lays a hand on your shoulder. "I don't know where you got that bike, kid, or how you got so good, but I know that if you keep this up you've got a good chance of winning the Tour of America."

Most of the bikers clap you on the back and congratulate you, but a few seem resentful. "There's got to be something special about that bike," one guy says. "I'd sure like to know what it is."

"It's just incredibly well made," you say.

Turn to page 68.

What could have gone wrong? Suddenly the answer comes to you. The lightning bolt must have demagnetized the air magnet! There's no way of fixing it during the race. You realize that although you probably have the best bike in the country, it's no longer a Superbike.

At that moment you look over your shoulder. The biker who stopped to help you earlier is gaining on you again. He must have gotten his second wind. And there's another racer behind him coming on fast.

You can't waste time moaning about what happened. You've got to get moving.

Turn to page 55.

You can't help feeling a little depressed. You still love biking, and you've got a great bike, but you know that without the air magnet you don't have a chance at winning the Tour of America this year.

You're tempted to stay in bike camp anyway. You'd still like to become a world-class racer, and it's the best training you could get anywhere. Besides, there's a slight chance the thief might be caught and you'd get your air magnet back. On the other hand, maybe you should drop out. You're not looking forward to telling Dr. Kepler about the theft, but maybe if you explain what happened, he'll give you a new air magnet.

If you stay on in bike camp, turn to page 115.

If you drop out and pay a call on Dr. Kepler, turn to page 53.

"Okay, thanks. I'll take you up on that ride," you say.

The officers drive you up the mountain and let you off at the diner at Loveland Pass, where you got kidnapped. You go into the diner to get something to eat.

Just as you sit down, you see a familiar face at the checkout counter. It's Pierre Le Beau. He waves at you as he leaves the diner. You watch through the window as he gets on his bike and pushes off.

You gulp down your meal and take off after him.

The final stretch of the race has some flat areas, but most of it is long grades up or downhill. Some of them are very steep, and you know that they're the ones Le Beau likes best.

But you've learned a lot about biking during the course of the race, and you're in even better shape than you realized. On the first straightaway you pass Le Beau. He tries to get into your wind shadow, but you manage to foil his attempt with an all-out burst of speed.

Le Beau is never far behind you throughout the final stretch. He gains going up the steep slopes, but he can't quite catch you.

The sun is dropping behind the ridges to the west when you finally cross the finish line—*first!*

Reporters and photographers throng around you. A cheer goes up from the crowd.

Turn to page 111.

TOUR of
USA
COMES
A
SUPPLIERS.
SILVER SPRINGS.

You quickly decide that there's no point in trying to talk to these guys. You know they mean trouble. You come down hard on your right pedal, then on your left. Your bike jolts forward, spinning the stick around. Fred, trying to hold on to it, slips sideways. At the same time Mack jams his stick forward, accidentally hitting Fred as he falls. By this time you're free of the stick and accelerating down the road. You look back and can't help laughing. Fred has gotten up and is taking a swing at Mack. The last thing you see before you turn the corner is Mack slugging Fred in return.

You sail down the next street, whistling a tune. You're sure happy to be rid of those guys. And what a bike! It's even better than you realized.

Just the same, you're going to have to think hard about whether to ride it to school again. You've got bigger plans in mind for the Superbike. You want to start training for the big tours and become a championship racer!

Turn to page 35.

The scientist leans toward you, looking very serious. "Pollution has become such a huge problem on this planet that life itself is threatened. And it's getting worse all the time. This trend can only be stopped if people become much more energy efficient, and the air magnet could be a big step in that direction. If more people would ride bikes instead of driving cars it would make a huge difference."

"But do you really think people would go for that?" you ask.

"Biking is fun," Kepler replies. "It could become people's primary means of transportation if bikes were faster and easier to pedal than they are now. I've decided that everybody should have the chance to own a Superbike. Once I disclose the formula and license my invention, Superbikes will be the only ones made."

"That'll be terrific," you say. "I'll want to get another one myself."

Kepler stands up. "Now if you'll excuse me, I want to get right to work." He holds out his hand to shake yours. "Thank you for testing the air magnet," he says. "History will show that you played a vital role in making Superbikes standard throughout the world. I guarantee that the first one off the production line will have your name on it."

The End

You're just too disheartened to stay at bike camp. You've made some good friends there, but the idea that one of the bikers stole your air magnet makes you pretty uncomfortable. You know that the chances of ever getting it back are practically zero, and without it you're no match for most of the other riders at the camp. You decide to drop out.

The day after you get home you bike over to Dr. Kepler's house.

The doctor opens the door when you knock. His eyes fall on your bike. "The air magnet's gone," he says.

"Stolen at bike camp," you say. "Sawed off."

You expected Kepler to be outraged, but he calmly bends over and examines the spot in the middle of the handlebars where the air magnet was attached. Then he pulls out a strong magnifying glass and peers through it.

"The microwires were severed. There's no way they could be repaired," he says. "Whoever stole the air magnet will never be able to use it. I'm sure he'll never even guess how it worked."

"Well that's some consolation," you say, "but not much."

Kepler motions with his hand. "Bring the bike in and leave it in the entry hall," he says.

The scientist leads you into his study. He motions toward an armchair. "Have a seat."

You sit down, and Kepler settles into a rocking chair. He takes out a pipe but doesn't light it.

Turn to page 31.

The next morning you and Tim wait in a drugstore across the parking lot from the video rental place. An unmarked police car is parked near the other side of the lot. The police have agreed that if Tim spots the thief, you'll come out of the store and wave at the plainclothes cop. You've brought a camera along in case it might come in handy.

Nothing happens all morning. Then, about a quarter to twelve, the police car pulls up alongside the drugstore. Its lights are flashing. You run out to see what's going on.

"Sorry kid, I got an emergency call," the cop calls. He guns the engine, and the car races out of the lot, siren wailing. You just have to hope the thief doesn't show up before the police officer returns.

Turn to page 19.

Four hours and twenty minutes later, you cross the Tour New England finish line at Kittery Point, Maine, finishing fourth.

You feel terrible, but several people come up to congratulate you. "Great race," they say.

"But I didn't win," you say.

"Yes, but fourth out of a field of five hundred is terrific! Especially for your first big race."

You accept their congratulations, but you can't help thinking that if you hadn't had a Superbike for most of the race, you probably wouldn't have come in fourth, or even fortieth.

That night there's a big party for all the racers. You meet lots of people and make new friends. Everyone agrees it was a great race and that competitive biking is a great sport.

Several people say they hope you'll be in the Tour of America next month. You tell them you will. Whether you can get your air magnet fixed or not, you're determined to become a champion.

The End

You decide to pass up bike camp and get some real racing experience under your belt. You register for the Tour New England, a two-hundred-mile race that begins in Rhode Island and continues through Connecticut, Massachusetts, Vermont, New Hampshire, and Maine. A field of five hundred bikers will be competing for the first prize of ten thousand dollars.

The race begins at sunup on June 21, the longest day of the year. The sun rises a little after 5:00 A.M. that morning in Newport, Rhode Island, where the race begins.

When the big day arrives, you and the other bikers form a dense pack near the ramp to the bridge across Narragansett Bay. You check your supplies—water, snacks, sunblock—and strap on your goggles. You're near the rear of the pack, but that doesn't bother you. Your starting position won't make much difference in a two-hundred-mile race. The sun peeks above the horizon between two church spires in Newport and casts an early morning glow on the choppy waters of the bay. It's a beautiful day, but you can tell already that it's going to be a hot one. This race may turn out to be more a test of endurance than of speed.

The starting pistol fires, and the lead bikers push off.

Turn to page 73.

You decide to wait. The others shouldn't be far behind, and one of them is bound to know which way to turn.

The minutes tick by. No one shows up. You look nervously at your watch, then back down the dirt road. Finally you can't stand waiting anymore. You bike back to the last rise to see if you can see anyone coming. When you get there you wait almost another five minutes before you spot a lone rider approaching. As he gets closer you see it's Jose Montoya.

"What took you so long?" you yell when he gets close enough to hear you.

He pulls up beside you and stops. "Cliff hit a ditch in the road and took a bad spill. I had to take care of him until a farmer drove by and called an ambulance. How come you're waiting here?"

"The highway's over the next rise," you say, "but the marker is down and I didn't know which way to turn."

Jose pulls out his map. "Why, it's a right turn, of course."

Turn to page 78.

At last you see a sign. You have to get quite close to it to read it in the semidarkness. It says:

WELCOME TO VERMONT

Vermont? You've been going the wrong way! You brake to a stop and check your watch. It's two minutes before nine, and you have the whole state of New Hampshire to cross in the dark! You realize that it's a hopeless task, even for the Superbike.

You turn around and pedal slowly toward a nearby farmhouse to use the phone. You sure blew this race, first falling asleep for three hours and then taking the wrong turn. Now you won't be eligible for the Tour of America.

You decide that from now on you're going to be smarter. You may not win any championships this year, but there's always next year. And the first thing you're going to do when you get home is learn how to read road maps!

The End

WELCOME
TO
VERMONT
THE
GREEN MOUNTAIN
STATE

You immediately grab your bike and hit the road. You hope you can make up the time you lost by falling asleep. Quickly you work up to thirty miles an hour, which is the highest speed this back road will take. You gain rapidly on the biker ahead of you, then you lose sight of him as he goes over the crest of another hill.

When you reach the crest, you see him turning onto a dirt road heading east. There's a flag flying at the intersection. Still pedaling, you check your map and see that the route turns here and follows a rough, hilly dirt road for ten miles before intersecting with another paved road that will take you into New Hampshire.

You speed down the hill, then brake for the turn onto the dirt road. The other biker is now only a few dozen yards ahead of you, but you know there's little chance of passing him at the moment. The road is too uneven and bumpy to risk going over fifteen miles an hour.

It's frustrating. You really want to catch up to the biker in front of you, but you're going to have to be patient.

A clap of thunder rumbles overhead. A strong wind comes up out of nowhere. Scattered drops of rain make dark spots on the packed dirt of the road.

Go on to the next page.

Out of the corner of your eye you see a flash of lightning. It's followed by another clap of thunder, and with that it begins to pour.

Peering ahead through sheets of rain, you spot an old barn just a hundred yards down the road. You wonder whether you should take shelter there or try to ride out the storm. You've been sleeping all afternoon, and you don't need to rest. Further delay might cost you the race. On the other hand, getting hit by lightning could cost you your life!

If you keep going, turn to page 76.

If you take shelter, turn to page 67.

You can hardly believe it! You've won the Tour New England trophy and the ten-thousand-dollar prize that goes with it, and you've got a good shot at the Tour of America coming up next month.

You pat the bike that took you through five states in a single day. It's a Superbike, all right.

Turn to page 74.

64

The man who was trying to bring you around sees that you've come to. He steps back, and you recognize him as the biker who was ahead of you.

"You all right?" he asks.

"I think so," you say, though you still have a headache. You stand up carefully and brush yourself off. "Where did you come from?"

"I stopped off in a barn when the storm hit. I thought you were going to duck in there, too, but you just kept going."

"Yeah, I guess I should have stopped." You look around. A gentle rain is still falling, but the wind has stopped. You can see a patch of blue sky in the west. Your head is feeling better every minute, and you decide it's time to get moving again. There's still a chance you could win this race. You pick up your bike and wheel it onto the road.

"You go ahead," you say to the other biker. "You'd be half a mile down the road by now if you hadn't stopped to help me."

"You sure you're all right?" he says.

"Yes, definitely, thanks, but please go on, because I want to get back in the race."

"Okay." He gets on his bike and takes off.

Go on to the next page.

You wait until he's covered about half a mile and then you push off, too. You pull abreast of him just as the two of you reach the end of the dirt road.

"Say, is there anyone else ahead of us?" you call to him.

"The only one I saw was Pete Gregory, the national champion. If Pete got caught in the storm, you might be able to catch him. Not me, though—I'm pooped."

Turn to page 84.

You want to win, but not enough to risk being killed by lightning. You duck into the barn. A few moments later the rain turns into a deluge.

In the dim light inside, you see six or seven cows and, sitting on a pile of hay in a corner, the biker who was just ahead of you.

"Hi there. I'm Cliff Andrews," he says.

You introduce yourself, and the two of you shake hands. A second later, you both jump as a tremendous thunderclap sounds over your heads.

"Lucky we found shelter," Cliff says. "That storm is dangerous."

You peer out at the rain lashing the hillside, then blink as a flash of lightning leaps across the sky. Another thunderclap follows. You turn to your new friend. "Say, Cliff, do you know if anyone's ahead of us in the race?"

"Just Pete Gregory, as far as I know," Cliff says. "If he got caught in the storm, too, we might be able to catch him when it lets up."

You glance at your watch, then look out the door again. You wish the storm would pass quickly. You're itching to get back on the road, especially now that you know there's probably only one biker ahead of you.

Then, through the driving rain, you see a figure. It's another racer seeking refuge. He comes in, dripping wet.

"Jose Montoya," he says.

"Hi," you and Cliff say.

Turn to page 92.

That afternoon you go for a ride up the mountain in a gondola, then take a leisurely swim in the heated pool. The mountain air and scenery are great. So is the huge steak dinner you're served that night, which is topped off with ice cream and fresh strawberries for dessert. You think again how glad you are that you decided to come to bike camp. You're sure that your experience here will make all the difference when the big race rolls around. Your last thought before falling asleep that night is, *I'm going to win the Tour of America. Nothing's going to stop me.*

The next morning you wake up and find that the air magnet has been stolen from your Superbike—cut off with a hacksaw!

You can't believe it. You keep running your fingers over the rough place on the handlebars where the air magnet used to be. Who could have done such a thing?

Turn to page 72.

You wake up with a headache, lying in a muddy ditch. A man is kneeling beside you, gently tapping your cheek with his palm. Slowly it dawns on you where you are—in Vermont, in a bike race. You must have been knocked off your bike by lightning!

About twenty yards away you see a tree that has been split wide open. That must be where the lightning struck. It's lucky you weren't any closer.

Turn to page 64.

Where is the flag? You're wasting precious time. Then you spot it. It's lying in the ditch in a puddle of water. The wind and rain must have knocked it down. There's no way of telling which direction the arrow was pointing. You're going to have to figure out which way to go on your own.

You quickly pull out your map. It's crumpled, but fortunately you were carrying it in a waterproof pouch. The map shows that the final stretch of road runs straight across southern New Hampshire to the finish line, just across the Maine border. You look at the road and then at the map again.

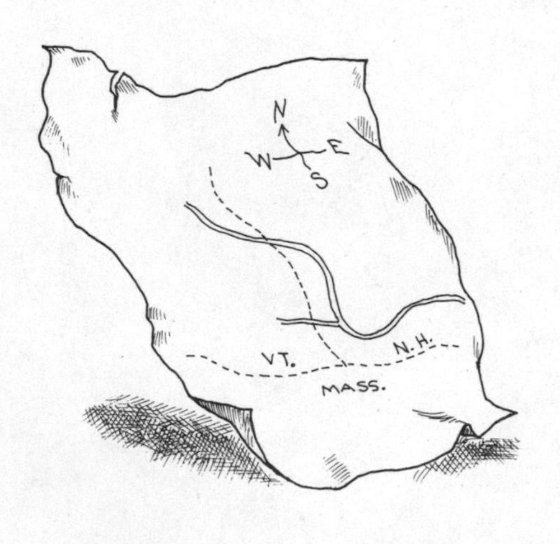

If you turn right, turn to page 82.

If you turn left, turn to page 79.

If you decide to wait for the next biker to catch up and see what he thinks, turn to page 57.

You report the theft to Ollie Strauss, the camp director. He immediately calls the police. An officer arrives about an hour later, and he and Mr. Strauss begin an investigation.

Not surprisingly, no one will admit to the theft, and unfortunately no clues are found. Whoever did the job was clever enough not to leave fingerprints. You have to face the fact that while your bike is still as good as any in the country, it's no longer a Superbike.

For the next two days you ride along with the other bikers, usually coming in near the rear of the pack. You can't stop thinking about the theft. You figure that whoever stole the air magnet probably tried to attach it to his own bike. Once he found out it wouldn't work anymore, chances are he hid it or buried it somewhere so no one would discover the evidence of his crime.

Turn to page 47.

You tell yourself not to set too fast a pace, but the Superbike seems to want to cover ground. You weave around the bikers ahead of you, passing one after another. About forty minutes later you cross the state line into Connecticut. By now only six or seven bikers are ahead of you, but you know they're some of the best in the world.

You cruise through Connecticut toward Massachusetts, taking the lead near Torrington, in the north central part of the state. A warm breeze blows at your back, and you hardly need the air magnet to cut your wind resistance to zero.

Turn to page 81.

When you get home, you stop by Dr. Kepler's house to give your report on his invention. You can't wait to tell him how well it worked.

He beckons you into his study and offers you a glass of iced tea. He listens intently as you describe the race, especially when you tell him how you overtook some of the world's top racers even after having slept half the afternoon and been delayed in a storm.

"Very good, very good," he keeps saying as you talk. When you're finished, he says, "The air magnet has performed exactly as I'd hoped. If you're willing to take some risk, there's a chance your Superbike will do something even more spectacular."

"More spectacular than winning a biking trophy? What's that?"

"Simply this, my young friend. The air magnet diverts the air in the bike's path, greatly reducing air friction as you move. Suppose you had a more powerful magnet and trained it straight up?"

You don't understand what he's getting at. "What would that do?"

"Don't you see? It would reduce the air pressure above you. That's exactly what happens over the wings of a plane. You'd have a flying bike!"

Turn to page 85.

TV cameras are lined up on the scene, and the mayor of the city is on hand to fire the starting pistol. The Parks Department band plays the Star Spangled Banner. The crowd cheers. And the race begins!

You manage to stay out of the crush crossing the starting line. Your main concern is to avoid a collision during the crowded start of the race. You pedal easily along near the middle of the pack as you and the other racers circle Central Park, then head toward Riverside Drive and the George Washington Bridge. You cross the bridge about thirtieth in the race.

You're not in too much of a hurry yet. The first few miles are for warming up and getting the kinks out of your legs.

Once across the bridge and into New Jersey, you really let loose. You shift into high gear and turn your air magnet on full force.

As you speed along the special lane reserved for the race, you pass one biker after another. About midway across New Jersey you break your personal record for speed on level ground, reaching an amazing fifty-seven miles per hour! Then you ease off a little. Though your bike has the best tires and the best balance of any in the world, there's always the risk of an accident at high speed.

Turn to page 88.

You decide you can't afford any further delay. You have to keep going if you want to win. You bike past the barn and start up a long hill. Rain pelts you. Lightning flashes around you. A crack of thunder sounds so close that you almost jump off your bike. Pedaling is an effort, even with the Superbike, because the road is getting muddy. Your bike's wheels splash through puddles and send spray flying on either side. You can feel the cold wind through your wet clothes.

You clear the crest of the hill. By now, you should have caught up to the other biker, but there's no sign of him. You figure he must have ducked into the barn you passed. You start down the slope, trying to pick up as much speed as possible even though your wheels are slipping in the mud.

The rain pelts down even harder. You can hardly see the road in front of your wheels. Suddenly a brilliant flash of light blinds you as a thunderous jolt throws you off your bike. You black out before you hit the ground.

Turn to page 69.

"Thanks," you say. "Excuse me, but I've got a lot of ground to make up." You push off and pedal for all you're worth. When you reach the macadam road, you turn right and accelerate, shifting up into top gear as you pass thirty miles an hour. A couple of miles down the road you see a sign that says:

MAINE BORDER 87 MILES

Jose gave you good directions, all right. The rest is up to you.

It's getting darker every minute, and you're forced to slow down. You can't risk hitting a rut or a stone when you're going fifty miles per hour. Still, it's only an hour and fifty minutes later that you cross the Maine border. A mile after that, the judges wave you across the finish line. Two people run up to help you off your bike and give you a blanket.

"Terrific race," one says. "You finished fourth!"

You take a long swig from a water bottle and head for the bus that will take you and your bike to one of the inns reserved for the racers.

You feel a little disappointed but happy at the same time. You didn't win the race, but you know that you and the Superbike make a great combination. There's one thing you'll have to do before you enter the Tour of America, however: learn to read road maps!

The End

You turn left and accelerate on the rolling concrete highway. The air magnet is working perfectly, and within seconds you hit forty miles per hour, then forty-five.

After a few minutes you notice that a car is following you. The driver honks several times. You wonder what his problem is.

You pedal harder, but the car keeps following you and honking. The driver seems to want you to stop. Maybe he's after your Superbike!

You put all your energy into pedaling, and a mile or so later the car turns off on a side road. You're glad of that, especially since you're going up a steep hill now and losing some speed.

When you reach the crest of the hill you have a good view of the road for two or three miles ahead. You strain your eyes in the fading light, hoping to catch sight of one of the bikers ahead of you. But the road is empty except for a pickup truck headed your way.

I'll catch them yet, you tell yourself, but for the next hour you bike on and on as if you were racing only yourself. Even though it's the longest day of the year, darkness is settling over the countryside. You have to slow your pace. At forty-five miles per hour, hitting a rut or a stone could be fatal, even for a Superbike.

Turn to page 58.

You race through the hilly country of western Massachusetts and cross into Vermont at about 2:00 P.M. You don't know how big your lead is, but you know it's time for a rest. You can't remember ever feeling so tired, hot, thirsty, and hungry. You stretch out on a soft, mossy bank in the shade of an old maple tree. After a drink of water and a snack of raisins and nuts, you lie back and close your eyes. Birds are singing in the trees, and bees are buzzing among the wildflowers along the road. It feels so good to lie down and rest.

Without meaning to, you drift off to sleep. You don't wake up until a loud clap of thunder erupts above you. You sit up with a start. Huge, dark storm clouds are rolling across the sky. You look at your watch. It's 5:00 P.M. You've been asleep for almost three hours!

You glance at the road and see a biker at the crest of the next hill. There's a number on his back. You're too far away to read it, but it's obvious that he's in the race. That means at least one biker is ahead of you now, and maybe more.

Turn to page 60.

You turn right and start pedaling, shifting smoothly as you pick up speed. A couple of miles down the road you see a sign that says:

MAINE BORDER 87 MILES

You're relieved to see that you're on the right road. Each time you go over the crest of a hill, you look for any bikers ahead of you. You don't see anyone for a while, but you know you must be gaining. The Superbike is really flying. Finally you pass one biker, then about a mile from the finish line you pass another. You know that Pete Gregory, one of the top bikers in the world, is still ahead of you, but you're not too worried. Pete is a terrific competitor, but you've got a Superbike! A few minutes later, on the curving downside of a long hill, you whip by him at fifty miles an hour.

You'd like to look back and see the look of astonishment on his face, but you don't dare. It's getting darker by the minute, and you have to keep your eyes on the road. A spill at this speed could be fatal.

Go on to the next page.

Darkness creeps over the countryside, but all you have to do now is maintain your lead. You practically coast the rest of the way. There's no way Pete can catch you now.

At 9:27, as the last bit of twilight is fading from the sky, you cross the finish line amid cheers from the onlookers lining the road. You hop off your bike and receive the handshake of the chief judge of the race. Someone comes up and gives you water and a blanket. Reporters crowd around you.

Turn to page 62.

You don't feel pooped at all. Your headache is almost gone, and you're well rested from your long nap earlier. You wave at the other biker and turn onto the macadam road that will take you to the New Hampshire border and then across the southern part of the state to the finish line in Maine.

You accelerate quickly, relishing the feel of the pavement beneath your tires. A glance at your watch tells you it's 6:00 P.M. It's the longest day of the year, so there should be light in the sky until after nine. There's still a chance you can make the Maine border before dark, and now you know there's only one racer ahead of you. It's true he's the national champion, but you're well rested, in good shape, and you've got a Superbike!

The road ahead is as straight as an arrow. You're determined to rev your bike to the limit. You pedal hard, shifting up as you pick up speed. You feel the bike accelerating, but something is wrong. The faster you go, the more wind blows in your face. You can't get your bike to go over thirty!

Suddenly you realize what's wrong—the air magnet isn't working! You fiddle with the knob, but nothing happens.

Turn to page 46.

"You see," Kepler says, "air pressure at sea level is about 15 pounds per cubic inch. Let's suppose that you and the bike together weigh about 105 pounds. 15 times 7 equals 105. Remove seven cubic inches of air pressure above you, and you are weightless."

The vision of millions of bicyclists soaring over the countryside fills your mind. It seems impossible. Still, you'd once have thought winning the Tour New England would be impossible, too.

"You don't believe it will work, do you?" Kepler says. "Well, trust me, it will. But it will take time to develop the technology."

"It sure would save a lot of energy if everyone had an air magnet," you say.

Kepler nods his head vigorously. "That's one of my most important goals," he says. "Look, you've proven your mettle with the Superbike. Would you like to be the first to try the flying bike?"

You're about to answer with a hearty *yes*, but Dr. Kepler is shaking his head.

"No, no. This is ridiculous," he says. "I should get a professional test pilot. This experiment is much too dangerous for an amateur."

You think about it. It does sound a little risky, but if things go well, your name will probably go down in history!

If you ask Dr. Kepler to let you test the flying bike, turn to page 112.

If you decide it's too risky, turn to page 99.

The announcer's words make you a little nervous. There might be some people who would like to look at your bike whom you wouldn't want to meet.

The next morning you leave at sunup and start your ascent. You're in terrific shape, and you make steady progress up the steep, winding road. After a few hours, however, you begin to run out of steam. You're exhausted when you reach the diner at the top of the pass. The altitude marker says 11,972 feet. No wonder you're tired! There's a lot less oxygen up here than there is at sea level. You need to take a break.

You turn into the parking lot, lock up your bike, and head for the door. Just as you reach it, a heavyset man wearing a lumber jacket comes out. Another man, who is slimmer but very muscular, is right behind him. You step aside to let them pass, but the first one stops you and flashes the handgun he has hidden under his jacket. Very softly he says, "Unlock the bike."

You have no choice but to obey. The men order you to load the bike into a van. They shove you in through the back door and lock it. Then they get in front and drive off.

It all happens so fast you can hardly believe it. You were on your way to victory, and now you're out of the race and your life is in danger.

The van wheels around in a U-turn and heads down the mountain toward Denver. You look out the tiny window in the back at the mountain you just climbed. All that effort wasted.

Turn to page 107.

BABY DOE DINER
COLORADO
R6726E

You cruise along at about thirty-five miles per hour, which should still be fast enough to catch the leaders. Within half an hour you've moved up to the number two position. A few minutes later you come in sight of the bridge across the Delaware River. Halfway over it, you spot Pierre Le Beau, the greatest biker in the world, the only one still ahead of you.

Well, you think, he beat me into Pennsylvania, but he won't beat me to Colorado.

After you cross the bridge you apply more speed. Within a few minutes you pass Le Beau. You hear a helicopter buzzing overhead. You glance up, and some people in the helicopter wave to you. Two cameras are trained on you, and you realize that millions of people have probably just watched you take the lead.

"Good going, Superbike," you say with a grin.

Turn to page 94.

It takes a couple of seconds for Pierre to get his arms free. That's all the time you need to pull away from him. He comes after you, but he's too far back to get in your wind shadow.

You pedal even harder, going as fast as you dare on the slippery road. The rain starts coming down in earnest. You look back and see that Pierre is thirty yards behind you. He's pressing you but not making an all-out effort to catch up. You figure he's playing it safe, maybe hoping you'll skid.

There's a pit stop up ahead, a McDonald's that's decked out with welcome signs for the bike racers. It would be a good place to wait out the rain, but you decide not to stop until you've built up a bigger lead.

After you pass the McDonald's, you look back and see Pierre turning in there. Now you can slow down a little, but you don't feel much happier. You're chilled to the bone, and you can hardly see through the rain.

About an hour later the sun comes out. You're completely soaked, since you never did get your slicker on, so you stop to change your shirt. Soon you're back on the road again, cruising at forty miles per hour. You're in first place and you aim to stay that way—all the way to Aspen.

Turn to page 102.

DR.
FLINN

You wake up in the hospital with an IV tube in your arm and your right leg in a cast suspended in the air.

A doctor is standing over you. "How are you feeling?" she asks.

"Not too great," you say.

She smiles. "You'll be okay. It's a good thing you were wearing a helmet. Otherwise you'd be on your way to the cemetery by now."

"What about my bike? Do you know if it's okay?"

"I'm afraid it's not," she replies. "Fortunately for you it took the brunt of the impact. It's totally wrecked."

You feel tears welling up in your eyes. "It was a Superbike," you say.

"It's a shame," the doctor says. "Now it's just a Superwreck."

The End

Cliff and Jose settle down in the hayloft, but you stay where you can see out the door. You don't want to stay here a moment longer than you have to.

The storm rages on for another twenty minutes before the rain begins to let up. You step outside. The thunder and lightning seem to have passed.

"Hey, guys," you yell. "I'm on my way."

A few seconds later you push off down the road. Cliff and Jose are right behind you. You pull ahead of them, but not as fast as you'd hoped. The deluge has made a mess of the road, and you don't dare go over ten or fifteen miles per hour.

After about fifteen minutes you pass a sign. You can hardly read it because the paint is so faded, but you make out the words:

LEAVING VERMONT

That's good news. You're entering New Hampshire, the last state you have to cross.

It's now seven o'clock. The sun is shining again, but it's about to set behind the mountains. You had hoped the dirt road would end at the state line, but it seems to take forever before you finally reach a rolling concrete highway.

You stop and look for a Tour New England flag. There should be one at the intersection with an arrow showing which way to turn, but you don't see it anywhere.

Turn to page 70.

By now you're pulling your bike out of the van. You look it over to make sure it's not damaged. The officer you've been talking to takes a look at it, too.

"So that's the Superbike," he says. "I've heard about it on TV. They said it's a sure winner."

"Not anymore," you say. "Pierre Le Beau is way ahead of me now."

"Look," the officer says. "We know you got as far as Loveland Pass before those guys grabbed you. It wouldn't be cheating if we gave you a ride back there. Then you might still have a chance."

"Gee, thanks," you say. "But I'm worried about rule 4. It states, 'Any contestant whose bike is transported by any means over any part of the course will be disqualified. There will be no exceptions to this rule.'"

"I would hope they'd make an exception this time, since you got kidnapped," he says.

You hope so, too, but you're still not sure. The judges would have to have a meeting in order to decide, and you don't have time to wait for that.

---

*If you decide to accept the ride,
turn to page 48.*

*If you decline the ride and try to catch up from
where you are, turn to page 98.*

Then you look over your shoulder to see how far back Le Beau is. To your surprise, you're staring right into his face. After you passed him, he slid in close behind you. You immediately speed up, reaching forty, then forty-five miles per hour. Le Beau hangs in behind you, keeping himself in your wind shadow. He may be the only biker in the world who could do it, but he's strong and skillful enough to stay only inches behind you. As a result he's not getting any more wind resistance than you are with your air magnet.

Mile after mile, whether you speed up or slow down, Le Beau continues to shadow you. At one point you slow to only twenty miles per hour, hoping Le Beau will pass you. If he does, you figure you can zip by so fast he won't be able to get in behind you again. But Le Beau doesn't fall for this ruse. He slows down and stays right behind you.

Turn to page 106.

The afternoon and early evening wear on. Soon it will be 9:00 P.M., and racing will be over for the day. That's all right with you. You're tired and cramped from a full day of hard riding. About eight-thirty you check into a hostel for the night, and Le Beau checks in right behind you.

The next day Le Beau shoves off at sunrise. You start soon afterward. Again you pass him, and again he slips into your wind shadow. The whole day passes, and you still haven't been able to shake him. And again you both check into the same hostel, this time in Indiana.

You know Le Beau will be shadowing you the following day, too. That night you try to decide how to deal with it. An idea comes to you as you look over your maps.

Turn to page 103.

Before you go to sleep, you catch the late sports news on TV and discover that everyone is talking about you. You're a hundred miles ahead of Pierre Le Beau, and the next biker is forty miles behind him. A lot of racers haven't even reached Colorado yet. You couldn't be happier.

Then the announcer says that some experts believe you aren't riding an ordinary bike. "There's something about it that's very special," he says. "It's a real superbike! How else could an unknown racer be almost a hundred miles ahead of Pierre Le Beau? One thing's for sure—win or lose, a lot of people will want to take a closer look at that bike!"

Turn to page 86.

You thank the officers again and tell them you'd rather try to catch up on your own. You take a long drink from your water bottle, polish off a chocolate bar, and take to the road again.

About half an hour later, soon after you've started up the mountain, you realize you're not going to make it. You're still shaken up from being kidnapped, and you're extremely tired. You were already worn out from climbing the mountain the first time, and trying to do it again the same day is just too much for you.

Turn to page 109.

"No thanks, Dr. Kepler," you say. "I want to enter the Tour of America with the Superbike. I'll be as happy as a person can be if I win that race, so I don't think I'd better risk my life as a test pilot."

You continue training for the Tour of America. You take your bike up the steepest hills you can find to improve your strength and stamina. You practice shifting until you can accelerate and slow down as gracefully as a gull. You study your maps so you'll be sure never to take a wrong turn.

Go on to the next page.

The race begins on July 1 near West Seventy-second Street on Central Park Drive in New York City. It's only 7:00 A.M. when you arrive at the starting line, but the park is crowded with onlookers. Only three hundred bikers have

qualified for this grueling race, and you're proud to be one of them.

You're wearing a small, streamlined backpack that contains a rain slicker, snacks, sunblock, mosquito repellent, and a toothbrush. Your water bottles are full. Your bike is clean and in perfect condition.

Turn to page 75.

After you cross the Mississippi River, you continue on across the Great Plains. Three days' travel brings you to a hostel at the Colorado border. You flop into bed and fall instantly asleep.

You're tired from the many days of hard biking. But you feel that you're in really good shape. You know you can't climb mountains as fast as Pierre Le Beau, even on a Superbike. But you figure you have a big enough lead to win the race, assuming there are no unexpected difficulties.

Late the next afternoon you see the hazy outlines of the Rockies. The highest peaks are covered with snow. The closer you get, the taller the mountains appear to be. They look impossible to scale.

That night you stay at a hostel a few miles west of Denver, at the foot of the mountains. You eat a nourishing dinner and go to bed early. You know that the next day will be the hardest biking of your life.

Turn to page 97.

In Illinois, which you should reach early in the morning, the road forks. Bikers can either take the southern fork or the northern fork. The two come together again about a hundred miles later, just east of the Mississippi River. The southern route is about twenty miles shorter, so naturally Le Beau will be expecting you to take it. If you turn north at the last second, he might be fooled and veer south. Then, if you accelerate quickly, he won't be able to get back in your wind shadow even if he turns to follow you on the north fork. The only problem is that if you take the longer route you'll have to bike a lot faster than Le Beau does on the shorter one. Otherwise he'll reach the Mississippi ahead of you and you'll be right back where you started.

If you try to shake Le Beau by taking the longer route, turn to page 108.

If you stick to the shorter route, turn to page 114.

You stop your bike. Pierre stops right behind you. You reach into your backpack and pull out your rain slicker.

"How long do you think this'll last?" you ask Pierre.

"Don't know. It's one of the things we have to put up with in our sport." As he says this he's pulling out his own rain slicker.

You nod and pretend to be slipping yours on. Actually you keep from pulling your arms through the sleeves. All the while you keep an eye on Pierre. When he gets his hands about halfway through his sleeves you hop on your bike and push off. You pedal as hard as you can, upshifting smoothly even though you're holding your bunched-up rain slicker against the handlebars.

Turn to page 89.

ECO PRODUIT

Le Beau is really getting on your nerves, but there's nothing you can do about it. You wonder if he's planning to stick in your wind shadow all the way across to Colorado. No biking is allowed between sunset and sunrise, so you can't even scheme to be up and off ahead of him in the morning. Well, you think, if he *does* keep this up, it will still only get him second place.

Le Beau must have guessed what you're thinking, because he says, "Don't worry, I won't be following you all the way across the country."

"That's good to know," you say over your shoulder.

"When we reach the Rocky Mountains," he says, "I'll leave you behind."

A shiver goes up your spine. You dread those long, steep climbs through the mountains. It's impossible to travel more than five or ten miles per hour up some of those grades.

Suddenly you realize what Le Beau's strategy is. Wind resistance is no longer a factor when going uphill. Pierre, who is much stronger and more experienced than you are, will be able to outpace you once he reaches the Rockies. You've got to build up a big lead before then. Otherwise, you've practically lost the race already.

All day Le Beau follows you up and down the rolling, curving highways of Pennsylvania. Whenever you stop for a break, he stops too. And no matter how fast you get back on your bike, he's on his just as fast, and back in your wind shadow.

Turn to page 96.

About halfway down the mountain, you see a lone figure biking steadily uphill. It's Pierre Le Beau. In another hour and a half he'll reach the pass. From then on he'll be traveling faster than ever.

There's nothing you can do about it. You're out of the race. And you've got more serious problems on your mind right now than cycling.

The van has reached the foot of the mountain, but instead of continuing east toward Denver, it turns south toward Colorado Springs. You try to think of a way to escape, but it seems pretty hopeless as long as you're locked in and guarded by two armed men.

As you're thinking this, a siren sounds behind you. Two police cars are bearing down on the van. The van swerves, then brakes to a stop. You lie on the floor in case any shots are fired. You hear the amplified voices of the cops ordering the criminals out of the van.

A minute later an officer unlocks the back of the van and lets you out. You glance over and see the two criminals bent over a squad car. One officer is guarding them with a shotgun while another frisks them for weapons.

"Thanks," you say to the cop who let you out.

"I'm sure glad we were tipped off to this," he says. "Those guys will be out of commission for a long time, but it's a shame you got taken out of the race."

Turn to page 93.

The next morning Le Beau settles in behind you again, just as you expected. You watch carefully for the fork. You reach it about 9:00 A.M. The split in the road is marked by a cement guard wall. As you approach it, you're careful to keep a steady course and speed so that Le Beau won't suspect your intention. Then, just a few feet before the divider, you turn abruptly and graze past it onto the northern fork. Le Beau streaks on down the road, staying on the shorter route.

Your stratagem has worked—so far. Now you really have to turn on the speed. Even with the air magnet, it's going to be tough reaching the Mississippi before Le Beau does.

You crank the air magnet to maximum power, and pedal as you've never pedaled before. Forty miles per hour, forty-five, fifty-five . . . you break your previous record and hit a fantastic sixty-one miles per hour. That must be the fastest a bike has ever gone on level ground!

Then you hit sixty-two miles per hour. You can't believe your speedometer. That may be why you have your eye on it, and off the road, just a fraction of a second too long. You don't see the tiny pothole in the road ahead, and you and your Superbike fly off the road and into the cement wall running along the shoulder.

Turn to page 91.

You stop at a burger joint and find that six bikers have passed you and that Pierre Le Beau is only ninety miles from the finish line. There's no hope now. You might as well sit down and relax. You order a hamburger, fries, and soda.

The owner of the restaurant brings your food. "This is on the house," he says. "It's a shame what happened to you. Everyone thought you were going to win the Tour of America."

"Well, I won't win it this year," you say. "But next year's going to be a different story."

The End

When you get home, you put your bike in the garage and lock it to a metal pipe that helps support the garage roof. Then you go to your room and memorize the lock combination. After carefully hiding the piece of paper, you sit on the edge of your bed and try to sort out your thoughts. Owning the Superbike is exciting, but it's also quite a responsibility. You wonder whether you should show your friends what it can do. You'd love to show it off, but you're afraid of what could happen if word got out about the bike's amazing powers. Maybe you should pretend it's just an ordinary bike and only race it out on the back roads.

If you decide to show your friends what the bike can do, turn to page 12.

If you decide to keep the Superbike's special powers a secret, turn to page 35.

However, your elation is short-lived. An official tells you that the judges are arguing with each other about whether you should be disqualified for getting a ride in the police van.

Twenty minutes later, Pierre Le Beau crosses the line. He spots you and comes over. "Great race," he says. "You're a real champion!"

"You rode a great race, too," you say. "And you may be the one who's declared champion!" You explain what happened.

"They want to disqualify you because you got a ride in the police car? But it was only over ground you'd already covered under your own power."

"I know, but—"

Just then an official comes over. He puts his hand on your shoulder, but his eyes are on Le Beau. "The judges have decided that the winner will be the Superbiker here, Pierre, unless you protest under rule 4."

"I'm not going to protest," Le Beau says. He holds out his hand to you. "My Superbiker friend here won fair and square."

The next minute a gold medal is being pinned on you. You're practically being dragged in front of the TV cameras.

"Here's the championship biker," someone says.

"Thanks," you say. Then you point to Le Beau. "And here's a championship guy."

The End

You beg Dr. Kepler to let you be the first to test the flying bike, and you finally convince him to let you try. Three weeks later you return to his lab, and he attaches a different air magnet to your bike.

"Please," he says. "The first time you use it, be very careful. And be sure to try it out where no one can see you. I want to keep my invention a secret until it's perfected."

"Sure thing," you say.

Early the next Saturday morning you hop on your Superbike and head out of town. It doesn't take you long to find the right spot for your experiment—a lonely pasture shielded from the road by a strip of woods. The whole area is completely deserted except for a few cows.

You wheel the Superbike to the center of the pasture. Then you sit on it and turn the knob on the air magnet.

You hear a hiss and feel a rush of air flowing around your feet, but you remain firmly on the ground.

Frustrated, you crank the knob as far as it goes. A great roar of wind rushes toward the ground. You and the bike sail into the air, higher and higher. You panic and reverse the lever. The next moment you're plummeting toward Earth.

The farmer who finds your body never figures out how you could have had a biking accident in the middle of a pasture.

The End

You decide that taking the longer northern route doesn't make sense. If it turned out to be a rough road, all the best bikers could pass you before you made it to the other end. You're better off following the shorter route and trying to figure out another way to shake Le Beau before you reach the Rockies.

You come to the fork about a half hour after getting underway the next day, and you veer to the south as you planned. Pierre hangs right on your tail. He's so strong and skillful that there seems to be no way of shaking him.

Shortly before noon it begins to drizzle. You can see a line of dark clouds gathering on the horizon ahead of you. It looks as if you'll soon be caught in a downpour.

Even a little rain makes the road slick. You have to slow down, and of course Pierre slows, too. Then you think of a scheme to shake him.

Turn to page 104.

You decide to stay on in bike camp. Although your bike is still the best in the camp, most of the other bikers are stronger and more experienced than you, and for the next week you're nearly always one of the last to finish. Still, you keep at it. You enjoy biking and make many good friends. And you get better and better each week. You come in sixth out of fifty in the final twenty-kilometer race, even though you're the youngest one in the camp.

At the big farewell dinner that night, Ollie Strauss, the camp director, gives a speech. He talks about what a great group of bikers have been at the camp and says that he's spotted three or four future champions in the group. Later he takes you aside.

"I really admire the way you stuck with it even after your air magnet was stolen," he says.

"I'm glad I did," you say. "I've had a great time. I only wish I still had a Superbike."

"You may not have a Superbike," he says, "but you're a Superbiker!"

The End

ABOUT THE AUTHOR

EDWARD PACKARD is a graduate of Princeton University and Columbia Law School. He developed the unique storytelling approach used in the Choose Your Own Adventure series while thinking up stories for his children, Caroline, Andrea, and Wells.

ABOUT THE ILLUSTRATOR

JUDITH MITCHELL was born and raised in New York City. She earned a Bachelor of Fine Arts degree from Chatham College and has also studied art at the Columbia University School of Arts and at the School of Visual Arts in New York City. Ms. Mitchell is the illustrator of *The Search for Aladdin's Lamp* in the Choose Your Own Adventure series. When she isn't working, she enjoys music, animals, cooking, collecting antiques, and traveling. Judith Mitchell lives in New York City.